King for a Day!

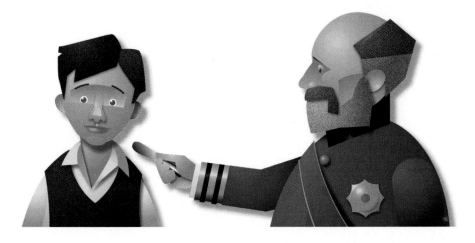

written by Justine Korman Fontes

illustrated by John Hovell

Macmillan
McGraw-Hill

New York   Farmington

"Someday this kingdom will be yours to rule!"
King Robert said to his thirteen-year-old son,
Prince Paul.

The Prince of Avalon was home from school
for the holidays. The royal cook had said that he
was "looking very tall and grown-up," but looking
tall and grown-up was one thing—being King
was another. Prince Paul was in complete awe
of his father.

King Robert continued, "You'll make a great King. It's your destiny!"

Queen Meredith's little black terrier, Pepper, barked as he always did when the King spoke. Queen Meredith scratched under the dog's chin, then she turned to her son. "Why don't you try being King for a day, and see how you like it?" she said.

King Robert took his butter knife and tapped it on Prince Paul's shoulders, saying, "You are now King for a day!"

Prince Paul felt the pancakes flip-flop in his stomach. "But I wouldn't know what to do!" Paul said.

Queen Meredith said, "Perhaps you had better let your father do all the work. You can watch, imagining yourself in his place."

That day, the King's first visitor was the ambassador from Elsinore, the country to the west of Avalon.

On their way to the throne room, King Robert tried to explain the problems between the two countries. "It all started with an argument over land and a treaty neither side thought was fair. Now...," his voice trailed off, "if we don't find a compromise, there might be a war."

Prince Paul was worried. What if Avalon lost? What would happen then?

Prince Paul watched his father speak with the ambassador of Elsinore, then with his counselors. Then his father prepared a new treaty for the Queen of Elsinore.

The Prince tried to imagine himself wearing his father's robe and sitting on his father's throne. Would he ever know how to make the right decision? If King Robert's treaty was acceptable to the Queen, his father would keep the peace. If it was not....

Prince Paul straightened his father's crown. As he moved in his chair, it would begin to slide off his head. Prince Paul didn't believe he would ever be the King his father was.

King Robert's next audience was with Sir Isaac Nautilus. Sir Isaac wanted to travel to a faraway island thought to have lots of buried pirate treasure.

"I'll need ships, a crew, arms, and supplies. Of course, if I am successful, I will claim the island for the kingdom of Avalon. I only ask for a quarter of the treasure in return," Sir Isaac said, with a sniff. "Does this suit Your Majesty?"

"It sounds great!" Prince Paul shouted. "Let's do it, Father—there's no telling what kind of wonderful stuff Sir Isaac might find!"

"I quite agree, my son. There *is* no telling. And the royal treasury is *not* bottomless," said King Robert.

"What can we do?" Prince Paul whispered.

"Let's try to interest some noblemen in backing the trip," the King said. "If the trip opens new trade routes and territories, it will make them richer than they already are."

King Robert and Prince Paul spent the rest of their morning listening to people ask for the King's favor or the money to build a new library, a dam, and an orphanage. Prince Paul heard case after case with his dad—after a while all the words and numbers mingled into a confusing mess.

"I didn't realize being a King was so much work!" Prince Paul groaned. His dad only winked at him and chuckled.

Later that morning, Prince Paul helped his father decide an argument over land. Despite their fancy clothes and fine manners, the two men resembled children fighting over the same toy.

Prince Paul was impressed by the fair decision his father suggested—it seemed no problem was too tough for him. Once both men agreed, the King spoke to them about Sir Isaac's trip. In the end, he convinced them to help finance it.

If that were not enough, at lunch more noblemen asked favors from the King. Prince Paul was getting upset because all the men were well-dressed and explained their needs so well. Deciding *who* was most deserving or *what* the Kingdom would pay for was terribly difficult.

After lunch, King Robert and Prince Paul
posed for a painting with the Queen. "Having great
works of art painted or plays, poems, and music
written is good for a country. This is also part of
the King's responsibility," King Robert explained.

Restless from posing, Prince Paul and his dad decided to go for a ride, so they left with a small entourage for the countryside. "Staying in touch with the common people is very important, too," the King said.

Prince Paul had a great time waving to the people. They stopped in small villages to accept simple gifts, such as flowers or homemade bread.

It was clear that the people loved their King and admired him for listening to their concerns. Just like the noblemen, they had lots of ideas on how to make things better in Avalon. King Robert listened just as carefully to them and had someone take notes on what was said.

"Their problems are just as important," the King told his son. Prince Paul nodded, feeling again the weight of the crown, even though he had left it at the palace.

Prince Paul was tired as they returned home, but the King's day wasn't over yet. The royal family was having a banquet for the royal family of Valhalla, Avalon's neighbors to the east.

"We must maintain good relations with them, especially if the Queen of Elsinore doesn't like the new treaty," King Robert explained to Prince Paul.

The dinner that night was followed by entertainment. "Other countries judge Avalon's greatness partly by how cultured we are, so we certainly don't want to appear feeble in that regard," King Robert whispered to his son over the music.

The Prince had almost fallen asleep when the Queen's tiny dog jumped out of her arms and scampered toward the gardens. Glad for a change of scenery, Prince Paul whispered, "I'll get him, Mother." Then, trying not to be noticed, he left the hall as quickly as possible.

Once outside, Prince Paul began looking for Pepper. The garden was cool and quiet, and the night air was filled with the fragrance of spring blossoms.

Rounding a flowering bush, Prince Paul came upon the Princess Pia of Valhalla walking with one of her ladies-in-waiting. Pepper was with the Princess, wagging his tail excitedly.

Prince Paul bowed to the Princess and picked Pepper up in his arms. The Princess scratched the little dog under the chin.

"I do hope my absence has not offended Your Highness—the meal was excellent and the music...."

"Do not trouble yourself with apologies, Your Highness. I, too, was more than happy to visit the gardens."

"There's only so much pomp I can take," the pretty Princess whispered.

Prince Paul nodded and smiled, for the Princess had echoed his sentiments exactly.

Just then, people came to the windows to watch fireworks in the sky above. So the Prince and Princess watched from a garden bench, as the lady-in-waiting stood nearby. As the guests cheered, the music started and people began to dance.

That was when the Prince asked, "If I were to write to Your Majesty, . . . would you do me the honor of writing back?"

"The honor would be mine," she said.

And so it was that the Prince and the Princess went back inside and joined in the dancing. The Queens saw this and smiled at each other. Then the King of Valhalla and the King of Avalon chuckled together and winked.